4 X'MAS

An Evening of Four One Act Plays

THE OFFICE PARTY
SANTA'S CLARA
BALLS
SANTA COMES TO THE KING DAVID
and
THE FIRST NOEL
a monologue

by George Cameron Grant

A SAMUEL FRENCH ACTING EDITION

SAMUEL FRENCH
FOUNDED 1830

SAMUELFRENCH.COM

MUSIC USE NOTE

Licensees are solely responsible for obtaining formal written permission from copyright owners to use copyrighted music in the performance of this play and are strongly cautioned to do so. If no such permission is obtained by the licensee, then the licensee must use only original music that the licensee owns and controls. Licensees are solely responsible and liable for all music clearances and shall indemnify the copyright owners of the play and their licensing agent, Samuel French, Inc., against any costs, expenses, losses and liabilities arising from the use of music by licensees.

IMPORTANT BILLING AND CREDIT REQUIREMENTS

All producers of *4 X'MAS must* give credit to the Author of the Play in all programs distributed in connection with performances of the Play, and in all instances in which the title of the Play appears for the purposes of advertising, publicizing or otherwise exploiting the Play and/or a production. The name of the Author *must* appear on a separate line on which no other name appears, immediately following the title and *must* appear in size of type not less than fifty percent of the size of the title type.

4 X'MAS first appeared in its entirety at the Jewel Box Stage of The Workshop Theatre, New York City, in December 2007 with the following cast:

*THE OFFICE PARTY
MAN . . . John Borras
WOMAN . . . Jerrah Kohn
RICHARD . . . Dylan Riley Snyder

+SANTA'S CLARA
SANTA . . . Philip J. Cutrone
KID . . . Dylan Riley Snyder
DAWN . . . Heidi Voight

+THE FIRST NOEL
NOEL . . . Mary Orzano

*BALLS
SILVER BALL . . . Joyce Lynn
RED BALL . . . Jessica Mazo
GOLD BALL . . .Linnea Peery
BLUE BALL . . . Kevin Rehill
GREEN BALL . . . Margo Singaliese

+SANTA COMES TO THE KING DAVID
TIM . . . John Borras
STELLA . . . Eileen Massmann
NURSE . . . Jessica Mazo
MARSHA . . . Margo Singaliese

Production's Movement Director: Bella Malinka

Directed by: *John Borras +George Cameron Grant

SANTA COMES TO THE KING DAVID was a finalist in the 26th Samuel French Off-off Broadway Short Play Festival, thanks to the following:

STELLA . . . Marlene Asher
TIM . . . John Borras
MARSHA . . . Cynthia Granville
NURSE . . . Suzy Harbulak

Directed by: Tom Avitabile

BALLS was a finalist in the 33rd Samuel French Off-off Broadway Short Play Festival, thanks to the following:

BLUE BALL . . . Vinny Duwe
SILVER BALL . . . Ann Parker
GOLD BALL . . . Sarah-Ann Rodgers
GREEN BALL . . . Margo Singaliese
RED BALL . . . Heidi Voight

Costumes: Michael Schloegl
Curtain Crew: Julie Abramowitz, Mary Orzano

Directed by: Vincent Bandille

THE OFFICE PARTY

(Christmas music plays as lights come up on…)

*(**SCENE:** A living room with a decorated Christmas tree upstage, sofa downstage facing it. Clothes are scattered around sofa.)*

*(**TIME:** 10pm.)*

*(**AT RISE:** sofa begins to rock as music fades behind passionate moans…)*

WOMAN. Ohhhh yes!

MAN. Mmmm…dear God, nooooooooo…

WOMAN. …ohhhh, yes, oh God, yes…ohhh…

MAN. …ohhh, nooooooo. Ah…ah…ahhhhh…

(…a woman's bare leg rises, then drapes over back of sofa…)

WOMAN. …yes…oh yes…oh yeeeesssss!

(…top of a Santa cap bobs in and out of sight…)

MAN. Noooooooo!

(…leg quickly disappears…)

MAN & WOMAN. Oh…oh…oh…ohhhhhhh!

*(…a car passes by outside as bare-chested **MAN** bolts up, wearing long, red Santa's cap and fake white beard…)*

MAN. What was that?

WOMAN. What was what?

MAN. That noise.

WOMAN. I didn't hear any noise.

MAN. Sounded like a car.

WOMAN. There's a street outside…on streets there are cars…mmm, come back here.

> *(...as unseen* **WOMAN** *pulls him closer, he blocks her hands...)*

MAN. Think we'd better stop.

WOMAN. For God's sake, why?

MAN. It's just so...dangerous.

WOMAN. I don't understand?

MAN. You know damn well what I mean...*(whispers)*...Richard.

WOMAN. I told you, there's nothing to worry about.

MAN. How can you be so sure?

WOMAN. I just am.

MAN. But what if he...

> *(...* **WOMAN** *bolts up from other side, wearing Santa suit top...)*

WOMAN. *(puts finger over his lips)* ...shhh...don't worry about it and come back down here.

MAN. How can you be so calm?

WOMAN. Calm? You call this calm? I'm freakin' dizzy from you.

MAN. Please don't make it so hard.

WOMAN. *(looking down)* Mmm...too late.

MAN. Ohhh, I love it when you talk dirty.

WOMAN. I have to have you now...it's been so long.

MAN. But what if he comes home? Walks in on us?

WOMAN. Ahhhhhhh! All night long you've been saying how much you need me, want me, so do you want to make love to me or not?

MAN. More than anything and in every possible way, but...

WOMAN. ...but?

MAN. But I don't want to start if there's even the *slightest* chance that Rich...

WOMAN. ...I'm telling you, it's OK. He won't be home before eleven, that gives us a whole hour...a wonderful, fabulous, dirty, delicious hour *alone.*

MAN. Half hour.

WOMAN. Fifty minutes.

MAN. Forty.

WOMAN. Forty-five.

MAN. Sold!

WOMAN. Come here!

MAN. Oh, baby!

> (…**WOMAN** *grabs* **MAN** *by neck and drags him out of view. Couch begins rocking back and forth…*)

WOMAN. Ohhhhhh, yeeeesssss…

MAN. …mmm…

WOMAN. …ahhh…

MAN. …mmm…I don't know.

WOMAN. *I* do…now, baby, *now.*

MAN. Ohhh, yeeeessss.

WOMAN. Oh…oh…

MAN & WOMAN. …ohhhhhhhhhh!

> (…*couch suddenly tips over, covering their clothes, as* **MAN** *and* **WOMAN** *spill out, rolling downstage, still locked in an embrace.* **MAN** *wears Santa suit pants,* **WOMAN***'s bare legs peek out from beneath baggy Santa suit top…*)

MAN. You're unbelievable!

WOMAN. I can't believe this is happening.

MAN. Would anyone?

WOMAN. Just another ridiculous office party I wasn't even going to.

MAN. Neither was I…cramped, smoky rooms…

WOMAN. …packed with loud, obnoxious people…

MAN. …with absolutely nothing to say…

WOMAN. …and every one of them with only one thing on their minds…

MAN & WOMAN. …sex!

> (…*they tear at each other…*)

MAN. I walked in expecting nothing and there you were, as if you'd dropped from a cloud and gently landed before me.

WOMAN. Hundreds of screaming, drinking, dancing lunatics packed in like sardines when suddenly, as if some unseen hand had swept them all away, the air became absolutely still and the room completely empty, *except* for you.

MAN. And you.

MAN & WOMAN. Us.

MAN. I never dreamed you could be this romantic.

WOMAN. I never was.

MAN. Or maybe you *always* were and I just never noticed.

WOMAN. How did I get so lucky?

MAN. *I'm* the one who's lucky.

MAN & WOMAN. We're *both* lucky.

    (*…they laugh and embrace…*)

WOMAN. And the most unbelievable thing of all? It's happening with you! Of *all* people, *you*…no one will believe a single word of this.

MAN. Maybe you should wait until you're sure what *this* really is.

WOMAN. I know what this is and I want to *shout it from the rooftop.*

MAN. There's a lot of snow up there, hope you don't get cold feet.

WOMAN. Not in your lifetime, mister, I've dreamed about this for too long.

MAN. You have?

WOMAN. You bet I have.

MAN. Me too.

WOMAN. I can tell.

MAN. Speaking of telling, when do we? Tell him, that is.

WOMAN. Tonight…right away.

MAN. Gee, I don't know…

WOMAN. …I can't bear the thought of spending one more
    lonely night without you.

MAN. But what about…

WOMAN. …Richard?

MAN. Richard.

WOMAN. He's a big boy, he can take care of himself.

MAN. What if he can't handle it…freaks out…what'll we
    do?

WOMAN. However he reacts, whatever happens, we'll work
    it out …together.

MAN. You really are sure about all this, aren't you?

WOMAN. Completely, and I'm not going to hide it from
    anyone, *especially* Richard!

MAN. Then there's no other way.

WOMAN. None.

MAN. We face the music.

WOMAN. Face to face.

MAN. I'm scared.

WOMAN. Shitless.

MAN. Me too.

WOMAN. Two shitless, lovestruck, reckless lunatics.

MAN. God, how I love this lunatic.

WOMAN. And I you.

> (*…they embrace as car suddenly approaches and stops…*
> **WOMAN** *pulls away…*)

> Shit!

MAN. What's wrong?

WOMAN. It's Richard!

MAN. What?

WOMAN. He's early!

MAN. I knew it!

> (*…they scramble for their clothes…*)

WOMAN. Damn, where's my skirt?

MAN. Probably with my shirt…wherever that is…hold it…

WOMAN & MAN. …here it is!

> (…*seeing her skirt peeking out from beneath sofa,* **MAN** *grabs and tosses it to her just as she tosses him his shirt, they put each on just as car door slams…it drives off.*)

MAN. Holy mackeral, I forgot to put on my…

WOMAN. …got 'em!

> (…*disappearing behind sofa, she pops back up with his briefs and skyhooks them to his waiting hands, which stuff them into his pants…*)

Mmm, nice bulge, Santa.

MAN. Please, no jokes while I'm in cardiac arrest.

WOMAN. I'll get you a bypass for Christmas.

> (…*they nervously clasp hands…*)

MAN. You sure you're sure about this?

WOMAN. Positive…and you?

> (…*he grabs and kisses her, when suddenly each realizes they still wear part of Santa suit…*)

MAN & WOMAN. Shit!

> (…*lock turns…they turn toward opening door…a teen-age* **BOY** *enters, dropping a duffel bag onto floor and stomping his snow-covered sneakers onto floor mat…*)

BOY. Brrr…yo, Mom, I'm home! Coach cut us loose early… sure could use something nice and hot to…

> (…*seeing* **MAN,** *he's stunned…*)

MAN. Hey, buddy.

> (…*the* **BOY** *turns toward his mom…*)

BOY. Mom, what's he…(*turns toward* **MAN**)…what are *you* doing here?

MAN. Would you believe *both* our companies had their Christmas parties at the same place tonight and…

WOMAN. …we sorta', kinda' bumped into each other, honey, and um…uh…what we're trying to tell you is…

MAN. …your Mom and I have decided that…

WOMAN. ...go ahead Bill, tell him.

MAN. I'm moving back in, Rich...I'm...coming back home...

(...after a long pause, he runs to MAN*...they embrace...)*

...Merry Christmas, son.

SON. I love you, Dad, Merry Christmas.

*(...*WOMAN *embraces them both as lights fade into...)*

(BLACKOUT)

SANTA'S CLARA

*(**SCENE:** The shadows of Port Authority. A recycling machine, words REDEMPTION CENTER printed across it, stands upstage right, a garbage can stuffed to overflow with trash and boxes of old clothes stand downstage before it. A broken wooden bench sits upstage left.)*

*(**TIME:** Dusk, on an unnaturally hot Christmas Eve.)*

*(**AT RISE:** A **STREET KID** in t-shirt and shorts fishes through the garbage can, stuffing a plastic bag with empties, as **MAN** dressed in a tattered Santa outfit enters stage left, bulging red sack slung over his shoulder. Sweat-stained Santa cap, faded Santa pants rolled up over his knees, **MAN** wears unlaced red Sneakers, his equally faded, opened Santa coat revealing the soaked red bandana tied around his neck above a dingy T-Shirt through which he sweats profusely. Draped around his neck are numerous pairs of worn-out, mismatched, laced together sneakers, as well as a pair of cracked and faded patent leather Santa boots looped over his wide, cracked, once shiny belt...)*

MAN. Ho! Ho! Ho! Merry...

*(...he approaches **KID**...)*

...Christmas. Hey kid...*KID!*

*(...looking up, the **KID** waves him off, resuming his search through the can...)*

This is Santa Claus you're passin' by here kid — *the real deal.* Don't you wanna' tell me what you want for Christmas? Last chance. Poor kid, how the hell can anybody get the Christmas Spirit in 90 degree weather? It's unnatural, I tell ya'.

*(...he again approaches **KID**...)*

MAN. *(cont.)* Whatta' ya' say little man? Tell old Santa what's on your Christmas list.

*(…the **KID** turns and kicks the **MAN** in the shin…)*

Ow!

KID. Buzz off, creep!

*(…the **KID** takes off as the **MAN** grabs his leg, hobbling around…)*

MAN. Holy Christmas, what's the matter with that kid, not like I stink or any…

(…he sniffs his armpits and winces…)

…jeez, that *is* pretty bad, guess I could use a little freshening up.

(…he moves downstage to an imaginary hotel clerk…)

…accommodations for one, my good man, and don't forget, I want that special single night Holiday rate – I'll be checking out first thing and…the name? You must be new here, name's Claus, S. Claus…*(somewhat irked)*…pardon me, there's no 'E' at the end of that!… Yes, that's it …Oh, why yes, thank you, I'd like that very much…

(…he slowly removes sack from his shoulder, wincing in pain…)

…*does* get a little heavy after a day like today…

(…lowering sack to floor, he removes a half-filled pint of whiskey from his coat…)

…a toast! To the orphaned memories of Father Christmas!…*(takes a long pull)*…Ahhh, that's sooooo good.

*(…wiping his lips on his sleeve, he yawns, stretches, then carefully lowers himself, face first, onto the bench, where he quickly falls asleep and begins to snore. A **TEEN-AGE GIRL** enters stage right, dressed from head to toe in black. A face with pierced nose and eyebrows, shredded tank t-shirt and arm tattoos are mostly covered by her long, straight black and purple hair. She wears worn-out sneakers and black tights torn at both knees. Lugging a*

stuffed backpack, she totes a filled plastic bag toward the machine, jolting the Man out of his deep slumber...)

MAN. *(cont.)* What the...? Who...who's there?...

(...struggling off the bench to his feet, he clears his throat and brushes himself off...)

Ho, ho, ho, Merry Christmas, Merry...

GIRL. ...great! Another drunken Santa Claus!

MAN. Your good will is overwhelming.

GIRL. You want good will, their dumpster's across the street, bad will?...*(rolling up her sleeves, she stomps toward him)* ...Take another step closer and I'll give you all you can handle.

MAN. Whoa! Back off there, little girl.

GIRL. Little girl?

MAN. My intentions are completely honorable.

GIRL. The last "honorable" guy I met tied me to a bedpost all night and tossed me to the gutter in the morning.

MAN. That's horrible!

GIRL. No, that's just the way it is. Most guys are about as hard to read as a stop sign, it's the ones who *pretend* they're something else, *those* are the ones I have to worry about. Unfortunately, they're also the ones I keep running into.

MAN. All this pessimism from such a little...*young lady...* now how about showin' Santa some Christmas Spirit.

GIRL. You mean like the kind I'm smelling on your breath?

MAN. Uh, um...I admit that with all the running around I do, sometimes a little "spirit-ual" motivation is required...

(...he tries to see whiskey level in bottle...)

...damn eyes, they're useless.

(...removing a pair of small, round wire-rim glasses from his inside coat pocket, he puts them on, then closely examines the bottle...)

GIRL. And what's with all the shoes, you some kinda' travelin' salesman or somethin'?

MAN. Salesman, no…travelin'? Let's just say it helps to rotate the footwear…never know when you're going to pop a hole.

GIRL. I didn't realize hiking was in the fake Santa handbook.

MAN. Fake? Such an unkind word, so judgmental…would you believe…

(…*looking up, he sees her and gasps, dropping bottle…*)

…dear God!

(…*he frantically rubs his eyes beneath glasses…*)

GIRL. What's wrong?

MAN. It can't be!

GIRL. Hey mister, you OK? You're not gettin' a stroke or heart attack or nothin', are ya'?

MAN. Same eyes…same mouth…and the mole…there's the mole.

(…*the* **GIRL** *quickly covers the cheek he almost reaches…*)

GIRL. Don't touch me – and stop staring at me like that!

MAN. It's you, it really is you!

GIRL. Me? Me who? And who are you?

MAN. All these years, all those shoes, and poof! I lift my head and there you are, standing right before these tired, bloodshot eyes.

GIRL. Better keep that hat off in this heat, old man, your brain's starting to broil.

MAN. My brain's never been better.

GIRL. Then tell me what's going on here.

MAN. I'm not so sure you're ready for the answer.

GIRL. Try me.

(…*with a heavy sigh, he sits on the bench…*)

MAN. I'm Santa Claus.

GIRL. Yeah, right.

(…she returns to the garbage…)

MAN. What I mean is, I'm *your* Santa Claus.

GIRL. And I guess your sack's just chock full of wonderful toys and goodies just for me.

(…he removes plastic bottle from sack and holds it up…)

MAN. I wish it were.

GIRL. Sure you do.

(…she fishes a bag of half-eaten burgers from the trash and begins devouring them…)

MAN. You're hungry.

GIRL. Mind your own business.

(…standing, he removes several bags of cellophane-wrapped table crackers from his coat pocket, offering them to her…)

MAN. Here, take these.

GIRL. Go away!

MAN. Please.

(…she hesitates, turns, then quickly grabs crackers…)

GIRL. Thanks…now why don't you get lost before I scream for the cops, alright?

MAN. I already am lost, dear girl…and so are you.

GIRL. Me? Lost?

MAN. Until right now.

GIRL. Really? Oh, I feel *much* better…*(looks around)*…sure picked a great place to find somebody.

MAN. Can't think of a better one…*findings* can happen any-where.

GIRL. *Findings?*

MAN. When a lost one's been found.

GIRL. Lost ones, *findings*…why am I listening to this?

MAN. I know you think I'm crazy, but…

GIRL. …think?

MAN. I found *all* my lost kids very quickly, but you, *you* were the toughest.

GIRL. *Me?* One of *your* lost kids? Look, mister, you are *not* my father, my father left me a long time ago.

MAN. I know.

GIRL. *No you don't!* You don't know *anything* about me, how could you?

(*...she begins frantically feeding bottles into machine...*)

I'm tired, I'm hungry and I'm getting real angry, so why don't you just take your wino Fairy Tales and...

MAN. ...you weren't *always* like this.

GIRL. Don't keep saying that! How would *you* know what I was like?

MAN. Because I remember one time when you were all bright eyes and a smile.

(*...turning toward him, she jabs an empty plastic bottle under his chin...*)

GIRL. You don't remember anything about me because you've never been part of my life and you never will be part of my life – EVER! Why am I even talking to you?

(*...she resumes feeding machine...*)

All I want is my deposit so I can get a little "Christmas Spirit" of my own, a safe place for the night...

MAN. ...anything you say, Dawn...

DAWN. ..and I'm not wasting another second with some crazy, burnt out...(*she turns to him*)...what did you call me?

MAN. I said...Merry Christmas, Dawn.

DAWN. How do you know my name?

MAN. You told it to me.

DAWN. I never met you before in my life.

MAN. Sure you have, you just don't remember.

DAWN. That's crap, complete crap!

MAN. And what a beautiful little girl you were...long, dark brown pigtails, cheeks full of freckles...here, see for yourself.

(*...reaching inside his Santa coat, he removes a crinkly, yellowed photo...*)

DAWN. Give me that!

(*...she reaches for photo, but he pulls it back, retreats to the bench and sits...*)

MAN. You can look, but you can't touch – not yet.

DAWN. Why not?

MAN. It's the rules.

DAWN. Rules? What rules? You're not making any...(*connecting with the image*)...hey, that's...that's me...on Santa's lap when I was...

(*...she studies photo closely, the MAN, then photo...*)

...holy...is that...really you?

MAN. Handsome devil, wasn't I?

DAWN. OK, so what if that is you...what are you doing *here* the day before Christmas?

(*...he pulls photo away...*)

MAN. I was fired.

DAWN. Fired?

(*...tucking photo inside his coat, he stands...*)

MAN. That's right, fired...bounced...canned...Mister Ho-ho-ho given the old heave-ho! I ended thirty-two Thanksgiving Day parades – began thirty two Christmas Seasons – thirty two! Then at the end of parade number thirty-two, seven years ago, I was taking the freight elevator to the North Pole when I was intercepted by a security guard who escorted me to the office of some angry little man who informed me that my Clausial services would no longer be required that Christmas Season, or any other for that matter. Someone else would be sitting on my gold and red throne... to be precise, the nephew of the parent company's new CEO. Ironic, isn't it, Santa getting fired by a parent company. But there it was, just like that…tossed to the gutter, just…

DAWN. …*(just)* like me.

MAN. Yes…just like you.

DAWN. That sucks.

MAN. As a matter of fact, you're right, it did suck. It sucked so bad that I took the elevator to the top floor, climbed the stairs to the roof and flung myself, suit and all, onto the big red star at Seventh & 34th. It was, I'm happy to report, a direct hit.

DAWN. But you're here, how did you survive?

MAN. I didn't.

DAWN. You di…wait a second, are you trying to tell me you're…

MAN. …yep, as a doornail.

DAWN. Jeez, does that mean I'm…

MAN. …no, Dawn, you're alive…a little lost maybe, but very much alive.

DAWN. Thank God.

MAN. Happy to hear it still matters.

DAWN. So does this make you some kind of Angel or Ghost or…

MAN. …let's say I'm just one lost soul reaching out to another…kind of a "Lost Claus for Lost Causes."

DAWN. That what you think *I* am, a Lost Cause?

MAN. Look around you, Dawn, there are more of you out there now than ever before.

DAWN. Why are you doing this to me?

MAN. Are you happy?

DAWN. I survive.

MAN. How sad…so young to just "survive."

DAWN. At least I didn't kill myse…*(looks away from him)*…sorry, that was mean.

MAN. No, it's the truth…*(he holds up the photo)*…do you remember what you asked me for?

DAWN. No!

MAN. No, you don't remember, or no, you don't want to remember?

DAWN. I don't know…can I have that picture now, please?

MAN. Are you ready to go back, back to who you were *before* you were lost? Back to this picture?

DAWN. Why do I have to go anywhere? All I want to do is get a closer look at…

MAN. …the rules?

DAWN. *(Stomping her feet)* Fine!

> (*…she suddenly grabs picture from his hand and bolts cross stage…staring into the yellowed image for several seconds, her eyes glaze over, her legs wobble, then suddenly stiffen, as she scales the photo in his direction…*)

This is stupid! You're just an old drunk in a disgusting, smelly Santa suit and I'm not listening to another…

MAN. …Dawn…

> (*…he picks photo up as she drops to her knees and covers her ears…*)

DAWN. …ridiculous word…

MAN. …Dawn…

DAWN. …not…one…

MAN. …*Dawn!*

DAWN. *(Softening, almost childlike)* …yes?

MAN. Who am I, Dawn?

DAWN. Who are you?

MAN. That's right, who am I?

> (*…she slowly looks up at the now beaming* MAN…)

DAWN. *(Now like an 8-year-old)* You're Santa…who else would you be?

MAN. Come with me, Dawn.

> (*…she accepts his extended hand, stands, and follows him to the bench, where he sits and motions for her to sit on his lap…*)

Sit, sit, come tell Santa what you'd like for Christmas.

(*...she sits on his lap...*)

DAWN. Please Santa, don't bring me any toys, I don't want any dolls, and I really don't need any more tea sets.

MAN. What *do* you want, Dawn?

DAWN. Don't you know?

MAN. Not unless you tell me.

DAWN. What I want – *all* that I want – is to be Clara in the Nutcracker, so I can dance for my Daddy and make him proud of me. Can you make that wish come true for me, Santa?

MAN. I'm sure your Daddy would be proud of you no matter what, Dawn, but if it's really *that* important to you...

DAWN. ...it is, Santa, it *really* is!

MAN. More than anything?

DAWN. More than anything in the whole wide world!

MAN. Have you been a good little girl, Dawn?

DAWN. Oh, yes, Santa, very, *very* good.

MAN. Then so be it! You'll get your wish, my dear.

DAWN. Oh thank you, Santa, thank you!

(*...she leaves **MAN**'s lap and runs down stage into a spotlight as he withdraws into shadows...*)

Daddy! Daddy! Santa's giving me my wish, I'm going to be Clara...(*her voice now dreamier and more trance-like*)... really! I'm going to be Clara...I'm going to be...I'm going...to my opening night...on this perfect day... standing...standing in my beautiful blue dress, tip of my nose barely touching the closed curtain...when will it open? Will it ever open? Oh God, everyone I love in the whole world is on the other side of it – Auntie Gen, Uncle Jack, Grammy Violet, Grampa Walter and...(*peeking through the imaginary curtain for a brief second*)...Daddy...oh, I love you so much, Daddy...I'm not even nervous...I want you to be proud of me...oh, thank you, Santa, thank you so much for...(*Nutcracker music begins*)...listen, there it is, there's the music – the curtain's opening…it's time…*I'm ready!*

(…*lights go down as* **DAWN**/**CLARA** *begins her Nut-cracker solo in spotlight…*)

MAN. *(offstage)* Your performance is flawless. And as the music fades and the curtains close, incredible applause fills the theatre…

(…**DAWN** *walks downstage to await curtain's reopening…*)

…curtains re-open! Smiling, cheering faces everywhere…and in the center of it all, at the foot of the stage before you, your Father reaches up and hands you *the most beautiful bouquet of Roses you've ever seen!*

(…*accepting a bouquet of roses from the shadows before her, she gracefully bows…*)

DAWN. I'm in heaven…the curtain closes and re-opens… applause …so much applause…applause so loud it almost sounds like thunder…maybe too much…thunder…the curtain closes one more time and…

(…*she looks out, squinting, as music fades…*)

…what was that? Thought I saw something…something wrong …there's something wrong…WHAT'S WRONG? The thunder's gone…it's suddenly quiet… spooky quiet…deathly quiet…I feel sick, so sick… sinking feeling…no…don't do that…please don't do that…keep it closed! PLEASE DON'T OPEN IT! DON'T OPEN THAT CURTAIN! DON'T OPEN IT! NOOOOOO!

(…*she collapses to the ground and lies motionless…after several moments, she stirs and slowly stands, brushing herself off while still clutching the bouquet…*)

DAWN. *(continued)* Everyone tells me…they never saw Daddy happier than right before he handed me the Roses until the moment he fell to the floor…

(…*extending the roses, she gently lofts them into the darkness…*)

...and as I tossed them into the hole that held him, I promised myself that I would never come back or look back – that I would never wish for anything *ever* again – that I would never dance again, dream again, and never believe in anything – or *anyone* – ever, ever, *ever* again, *especially*...

(*...lights up as she angrily turns to find herself standing before the* **MAN**, *now the greeting card Santa of every child's dreams – perfectly dressed, snowy white fluffy beard, and a brand new pair of laced together sparkling red sneakers draped about his neck...she immediately begins pounding on his chest...unflinching, he absorbs every blow calmly, her fury eventually fading as, exhausted, she falls to her knees against him. He places a comforting hand upon her head...*)

SANTA. My journey is over
     but yours just begins
The child that was lost
     has been found once again
With pigtails and freckles
     a quarter-moon grin
To find who you are
     you must know where you've been

(*...he removes the sparkling red sneakers from his neck and drapes them around hers...*)

So slip on these sneaks
     run as fast as you can
Make a wish, find a friend
     build a house that will stand
But don't ever forget
     every gem has its flaws
And one crack in the jewel
     doesn't make a Lost Cause

(*...removing the old photo of them from beneath his red coat, he offers it to her...she takes it...*)

SANTA. *(cont.)* Merry Christmas, Dawn.

DAWN. Merry Christmas…Santa.

> *(…they embrace…Nutcracker finale begins as* **SANTA** *guides her toward a waiting spotlight, then vanishes into the now darkening stage…a smiling* **DAWN** *grasps the sparkling sneakers to her chest, then gracefully pirouettes forward, as lights fade into…)*

(BLACKOUT)

THE FIRST NOEL

*(A **YOUNG WOMAN** enters wearing threadbare coat, hat, scarf, pants and sneakers, a hood from a sweatshirt pulled over her head. The china-white fingers peeking through the digit-less gloves she wears grip a corrugated board with HOMELESS FOR THE HOLIDAYS scribbled across it in one hand, a coffee cup filled with crinkled dollar bills and change in the other...she stares skyward, smiles, then suddenly, with a cautious start, turns forward...)*

YOUNG WOMAN. Sorry. Didn't see you there...*(she extends cup, then, with a disappointed grimace, quickly withdraws it)*...thanks. Brrr, it's so damn cold. Funny how it always seems to *just happen* – the cold that is – just sneaks up on you. You know it's coming, it always does, but one day you're walking around in a t-shirt and shorts, then the next...go ahead, say it. I see it, I see what you're thinking. What's a young girl like me doing out all alone on the streets so late at night in front of a Chinese take-out on Christmas Eve? Well I'm sure not here for the moo goo gai pan, which I'm sure is very tasty and, come to think of it, I *am* pretty hungry, but no, I'm here because of a name. Whose name? *My* name. My name is Noel. I know, I know, you think I'm saying that just because it's Christmas Eve and I'm trying to squeeze an extra dollar or two out of you, and that my real name is Peggy or Jessica or Marge, but if that's what I really wanted, this probably wouldn't be the best place to be doing that, would it? I swear, Noel is my *real* name. It was my mother's idea. Her name was Sally and she always hated it, so she wanted *my* name to mean something, to be significant, to matter, and since I was a Christmas baby – well, almost – 11:58 to be exact, she had the last scream of Christmas Eve and mine was the first on Christmas day – that's right, it's my birthday, or the end of it – kind of stinks being born two minutes before midnight, seems like it's over before it even begins – so how come I'm not gathered around a fireplace surrounded by family and friends singing happy birthday and Christmas carols, while stringing popcorn around the Christmas tree? Well, first of all, I'm not really a family and friends kind of girl, and second of all, because I'm here. I *always* come here…right here…same spot, same time, same day, every year. Most would call it a tradition, I just call it a *must* – I *must* be here. Why? For her…*(looking up)*…the woman who gave me my name, and the woman who couldn't wait until just before midnight – *two minutes before midnight* – every single Christmas Eve when, no matter where we were or who we were with – would scoop me up into her arms, rock me back and forth, and begin singing…*(smiling down on imaginary baby she rocks. Sings:)*…

> The First Noel,
> the Angels did say,
> Was to certain poor shepherds
> in fields as they…

…*(looking up)*…and the Joke of it all? I was supposed to be a New Year's baby, but – *SURPRISE!* – I popped out a week early, only my father wasn't one for surprises, not this kind, at least. "Doesn't matter when you were born," he would always say when she was done singing, "we made you on April Fools Day and you've been living up to it ever since." That's called a *zinger*, in case you didn't know. This had become their main form of communication. Cruel, little verbal attacks that at some point replaced the sweet nothings that must have been whispered in each other's ear at some point in their lives together, but never during mine. Unfortunately for mother, he was a master of the zinger, and eventually, whatever the subject, right or wrong, he would always win, *always* impose his opinions on the subjects within his tiny domain – namely my mother and I – and *always* in an angry and hostile way, especially to me. As a matter of fact, I never remember him *not* being angry with me. It was like I was a nuisance, an inconvenience, an intrusion, as if his life stopped when mine began, and he never let me *or* my mother ever forget it. It's no wonder she was depressed all the time. She'd just sit at that open window – 90 degrees or 8 below, it didn't matter – and stare out into – what? Who can say? She never did. The past she once had? The future she never would have? Or just space? Nothingness. I never knew, and I'm pretty sure she didn't either, but one thing I *did* know is that I loved being with her, near her. You'd never know it to look at or hear her, but underneath it all she was a pretty optimistic person, and somehow she always made me feel that no matter how bad things seemed or actually got, people were basically kind and good, and that if you believed in that goodness, somehow things would always work out for the best, even if only for the moment, and if you strung enough of those moments together, well, anything was possible. Unfortunately, that philosophy never seemed to apply to her, father saw to that. Fortunately, he always left early and usually came back late, so we had plenty of time to be together, before and after school. Peaceful, *non-zinger* time. Time to comfort each other, I guess you could say, when she wasn't staring out that damn window, that is. Sometimes she'd get so lost in that outside world of hers, I'd run out of the house, look up at that window she'd be staring out of, jump up and down, waves my hands and scream "Mother, it's me, your First Noel." Eventually she'd look down at me and, with that pretend smile of hers would say "Come inside, honey, you'll catch your death out there." I'd be down here dripping with sweat on a boiling hot day, and that's what I'd hear from the window... *(she looks up)...that* window...the window that used to be right up there, in front of our house, the house that used to be where this Chinese take-out is now. She died on my fifteenth birthday, was buried two days later in a creepy place called Valhalla, which I once saw in an old Kirk Douglas movie had something to do with Vikings, and by New Year's Day I was out on the street – for good. That's right. No life of zingers for me. No sitting by the window growing old, waiting for something that never was, could've been, or never would be. No more feeling like I was an April Fools joke, that my breathing was a bother, that my very existence was a nuisance. No, not me, *I* would take my chances on the street. It's not so bad, not really. Like mother said, most people are very nice, especially the tourists, and especially at holiday time. Sometimes I make twenty-five, even fifty, once even made a hundred dollars in one day – and I'm becoming one hell of a zing – I mean – singer…*(she grabs her stomach, almost falling to her knees)*…no, that's alright, I'm OK, I'm fine…*(standing up and stiffening)*… I was invited to a big holiday bash tonight – music, carolling, a fine turkey with all the trimmings – but I'm really not really a crowds and carolling kind of girl, and besides, I had to be here…*(looking up)*…to sing for her, the woman who gave me my name…*(She walks away, then, startled, suddenly turns her back on audience.)*… I'm so sorry, I didn't mean to block your doorway, I'll just step to one side and be on my…excuse me? You didn't have to…but…thank you…happy holiday to you too…*(turning back toward audience, she now holds a closed styrofoam take-out container, which she slowly opens)*…well, whatta' ya' know…moo goo gai pan…*(looking up, smiling)*…my favorite.

(BLACKOUT)

BALLS

(THUNDEROUS SNORING reverberates throughout darkened theater as lights come up on **FIVE CHRISTMAS BALLS,** *resting snugly side-by-side. From stage right are four female balls –* **GOLD BALL, SILVER BALL, GREEN BALL** *and* **RED BALL,** *then the one snoring male –* **BLUE BALL.** *An oversized candy cane protrudes from a large crack in* **GOLD BALL.** *After one rip-roaring snore,* **GREEN BALL** *stirs, then suddenly awakens…)*

GREEN. Holy moley, would ya' give us a freakin' break with that snorin' already? How can they sleep through that?…*(rolling against* **SILVER***)*…Come on, Sleepin' Beauty, wake up!

SILVER. *(stirring in her sleep)* Oh, no…no…please…don't let him hang me…I'm too old…I'm fragile…

GREEN. …aw damn, not another nightmare…

SILVER. …he's much too young, he'll drop me…

GREEN. …mmm, this one's a doozy…

SILVER. …oh no! Not up there! No…no…no…no…no… NO! It's much too high…please, I beg you, not that high, what if I fall? What if the tree falls? Somebody stop him, PLEASE!

GREEN. Come on, wake up!

SILVER. *(eyes shoot open)* Oh my, what…

GREEN. …you were just havin' another crummy dream…

SILVER. …where am I?

GREEN. In the same cardboard box you wake up in every year, where do ya' think?

SILVER. That was hhhhorrible…the worst ever.

GREEN. But now it's over, alright? Just relax.

SILVER. Relax? It's a sign, I just know it – you know what happens when I get these dreams.

GREEN. Yeah, ya' drive us all nuts!

SILVER. Thanks for the sympathy.

GREEN. I don't know what's worse, your screamin' or fat boy's snorin', but I swear, if he starts blowin' glitter again I'll…

(…*seeing* **GOLD**'*s condition,* **SILVER** *suddenly shrieks…*)

SILVER. …ahhhhhhh!

GREEN. What the…

RED. …uhhh…ohhh…ooo…

BLUE. (*lets out a monstrous snore*) …grrrraahhhh…

GREEN. …cripes, are you freakin' crazy?

RED. (*still half asleep*) Mmm, your hook, it's soooo big!

BLUE. (*snorting from a half sleep*) Humph! I won't do it!

SILVER. It's Gold, look at her stomach, it's crushed!

GREEN. Whatta' ya' talkin' about?

SILVER. I think she's…dead.

GREEN. You crackin' up, she's not…(*rolls forward to see a broken* **GOLD**)…jeez, you're right!

SILVER. It's horrible!

BLUE. (*half asleep*) Go ahead and stick me on that puny, needle less twig, I'll merely shake myself off.

GREEN. Poor old ball, never had a chance.

SILVER. And she's probably been lying there like that since January!

(…*she begins to sob…*)

GREEN. Pull yourself together, will ya'? We don't know that and besides, there's nothin' we can do about it now anyway…

RED. (*teasingly, still half asleep*) Oh, no, you're not stickin' that thing inside me, no way, no how – I won't let you!

(…**GREEN & SILVER** *leer at* **RED**…)

GREEN. So many hooks, so little time.

SILVER. Not one shard of dignity, just a useless pile of tainted glass.

GREEN. This is great! We're stuck between Old King Troll, the Queen of Tarts and a C.O.A.

SILVER. C.O.A?

GREEN. "Crushed on Awakening."

BLUE. *(still to himself)* Go ahead, I dare you…

SILVER. "Crushed on…," where do you get this stuff?

GREEN. There are some things I just know, OK?

BLUE. …you'll never break me, *never!*

SILVER. Baloney! You heard it where you hear everything… on that stupid box out there…that…that…TV thingy.

GREEN. Hey, listen honey, I'm not just another dopey, mindless ornament hangin' on a pine tree for five weeks out of the year lookin' pretty like you jokers, I keep *my* eyes and ears *wide* open…by the time they pull that cover back over us, I've learned some stuff and if you were smart, you'd do the same.

RED. No…no…noooohhh – yes, yes, oh, *YEEESSS!*

GREEN. Love a girl who puts up a fight.

RED. Yes…oh, yes…deeper…deeper…*DEEPER!*

BLUE. …I require sufficient personal space around me…

SILVER. Alright, Miss Know-it-all, what are we going to do about our shattered companion?

GREEN. First thing we're gonna' do is have a wakeup call. *Everybody up…rise and shine!*

(…she emits a glass-shattering whistle…)

SILVER. Careful, you'll shatter us all!

BLUE. *(opening his wincing eyes)* Ahhh! What's wrong? Who did that? Why I'll…

GREEN. …you'll what, tubbo?

BLUE. It's you! Why, I should've known…consider yourself reported!

GREEN. Oooh, you're scarin' me…flake off, bulb boy!

SILVER. Could somebody tell me how a style less, arrogant blue bore like this survives year after year while our dear friend rests before us in a million pieces?

BLUE. Because, O fragile one, I'm *melamine*…unbreakable…an everlasting tribute to the marriage of style, science and…

GREEN. …*(and)* one day there'll be nothin' left but you and the roaches, I know, I know.

SILVER. What did the roaches ever do to deserve *him?*

BLUE. Go ahead and have your fun, but you've got less than a year before that cheesy silver pigment of yours begins flaking off your insides and slowly makes its gravitational descent to that inordinately rotund, glass bottom of yours.

SILVER. How dare you!

GREEN. Look who's talkin'!

BLUE. Then everyone will see through you like I do, and before you can say Fortunoff, you'll be in the trash with yesterday's twisted, knotty tinsel!

SILVER. You opaque, glassless bastard!

GREEN. Alright, you two, that's enough…we've got ourselves a little trouble here…see for yourself!

(…*she gestures toward* **GOLD**…)

BLUE. *(seeing* **GOLD** *and wincing)* Eeew! How unpleasant.

SILVER. Unpleasant? It's tragic.

BLUE. Not to diminish the sentiment of the moment, but these things do happen all the time – to *your* kind, that is.

SILVER. Well, it's never happened to one of *us.*

RED. *(starting to awaken)* Oooh…don't stop, don't…

(…*they turn toward* **RED**…)

GREEN, SILVER & BLUE. …wake up!

RED. Ah!…*(startled, she opens her eyes and looks around)*…uh hum…it's that time already? What's everybody starin' at?

GREEN. Hate to interrupt your amorous off-season escapades, but somethin's come up…

SILVER. …something horrible.

BLUE. Gold's dead.

(…**RED** *looks at* **GOLD** *and yawns…*)

RED. Mmm…tough break.

GREEN. Tough break?

SILVER. Is *that* all you have to say?

RED. No…*good riddance!*

BLUE. Now *there's* a ball with a heart of gold.

SILVER. How can you be so cold?

RED. Easy…she was a ballbuster.

BLUE. What do you expect from such a cheap – bauble?

RED. Kiss my seam, slimeball!

GREEN. Alright, so she wasn't exactly the Sugar Plum Fairy, but…

BLUE. …I can't believe I have to endure another holiday season on the same tree with this junk pile of common, five and dime, bargain basement ornamentation.

RED. Who you callin' common, you…you…*biohazardous blowhard!*

GREEN. Ahem…excuse me, you two, but…

BLUE. …blowhard? Tough talk coming from the only ball in town who personally knows how many hooks come in a box.

GREEN. Can we deal with the situation we have here… PLEASE!

(…**RED** *and* **BLUE** *snarl and hiss at each other as* **GREEN** *suddenly looks outward…*)

SILVER. All these years we've lived in the same carton with her and now she's gone…we'll never hear another syllable of her…

RED. …winey, complainin', pain-in-the-glass bellyachin' *ever again!*

(…*noticing something out front, a look of concern comes over* **GREEN**'s *face…*)

SILVER. How could you?

GREEN. Guys?

BLUE. Talk about the stand calling the tree green.

RED. *(to* **BLUE,** *menacingly)* Who knows, blimpball, maybe *you'll* be next.

SILVER. *(to* **RED***)* You're despicable!

> *(…* **GREEN***'s eyes widen in horror…)*

GREEN. Hey, guys?

BLUE. She threatened me, you heard that, *she threatened me!*

> *(…a look of panic is etched on gulping* **GREEN***'s face…)*

GREEN. Uh, excuse me, everybody…

SILVER. …if I didn't know any better…

GREEN. …guys!

BLUE. You're a witness, if anything happens to me, you'll know who to blame!

> *(…* **GREEN** *loses it…)*

GREEN. *KNOCK IT OFF, ALL OF YA'!*

> *(…a startled* **SILVER, BLUE** *and* **RED** *turn toward* **GREEN***…)*

RED. What's with all the screechin'?

GREEN. We've got problems…*big* problems!

SILVER. Did you hear what she said to Blue?

BLUE. That's right, did you hear what she said to…

GREEN. …I'll answer *your* question if you answer *mine.*

RED. This is a bore, I'm going back to sleep.

SILVER. Thank God…

BLUE. …for small favors.

GREEN. Could somebody tell me why they'd be havin' a St. Patrick's Day parade in December?

BLUE. They wouldn't.

RED. Don't be silly.

SILVER. Where do you see…

GREEN. …right over there…on that "stupid box"?

(…the others turn toward same spot…)

RED. Look, she's right.

BLUE. That's…odd.

*(…***SILVER*** *looks sideways…)*

SILVER. Look! Our shamrock friends are gone.

RED. *(sadly)* Their box is empty.

BLUE. That's because they're all out *there*, hanging on the windows.

GREEN. Why would they take us out in the middle of March?

RED. And just when I was havin' such a comfy…sleep.

(…they suddenly turn to another spot before them…)

GREEN. Shhh! Here they come!

SILVER. What's happening?

BLUE. Maybe we'll get some answers.

RED. What's the question?

SILVER. They look *real* upset…

(…they all gasp…)

RED. …why are they screaming?

GREEN. This doesn't look good.

BLUE. They're divvying up their possessions.

SILVER. They've never screamed at each other before.

GREEN. Not like *this*.

RED. They're really goin' at it.

BLUE. This appears to be very serious indeed.

RED. Sure doesn't look like that "chase me" game they play around the tree.

GREEN. Maybe that's because there *is no tree!*

SILVER. I just had a horrible thought.

RED. Oh, great.

SILVER. What if they…

GREEN. …look out!

(...they all duck...to the sound of glass SHATTER-ing...)

BLUE. That was close!

(...a large, broken angel wing lands before them...)

SILVER. Angel! They just killed Angel!

RED. They've flipped out!

GREEN. This is no time to panic. Think...what can we... *stems down!*

(...they duck again as glass shatters...)

BLUE. Now that was *too* close.

RED. I wanna' go back to sleep!

GREEN & BLUE. Would you shut up!

SILVER. What happens if they break up? They won't want us anymore.

BLUE. She's right, we'll be the first to go.

RED. We're gonna' wind up in the garbage with Goldie over there.

GREEN. We gotta' make 'em stop...somehow make 'em change their...LOOK OUT!

*(...they turn away and scream as a large clump of tinsel conks **GOLD BALL** on stem...she suddenly begins to sing...)*

GOLD. "...sleep in heavenly peace."

GREEN. What the...

SILVER. ...she's alive!

BLUE. Incredible!

RED. No way!

*(...**GOLD BALL**'s eyes shoot open...)*

GOLD. Uh..uh...what's wrong? What's everybody staring at?

GREEN. We thought you were...

RED. *(looks at **GOLD**'s stomach)*...dead.

GOLD. Dead? Don't be ridic...*(sees her stomach)*...ahhh!

SILVER. You were crushed by a candy cane, dear.

BLUE. This is how we found you, so naturally we assumed you were…

GREEN. …hold it! They stopped.

GOLD. Who stopped? What's going on, I'm getting scared.

GREEN. *You're* gettin' scared? I'm rollin' in a pile of my own glitter.

SILVER. They've been fighting.

GOLD. *Them?* Fighting?

BLUE. Hurling things at each other.

SILVER. Like a pair of lunatics.

GREEN. Which explains the candy cane.

GOLD. They almost killed me!

RED. Yeah…almost.

GREEN. Then suddenly they stopped.

RED. But why?

GOLD. And why are they fighting?

GREEN. We don't know that yet, but…

BLUE. …there they go again!

GREEN. Look out!

(*…they duck…more breeaking glass…*)

GOLD. What are we going to do?

GREEN. Wish I knew.

RED. I wanna' go back to sleep.

SILVER. They were really going at it until you started…

GREEN, SILVER & BLUE. …singing!

GREEN. That's it!

SILVER. What's it?

BLUE. The reason they stopped fighting.

GOLD. I'm confused.

GREEN. *They* stopped fighting when *you* started singing.

BLUE. So the logical conclusion would be…

GREEN. …we sing for our lives!

SILVER. Then what are we waiting for?

RED. You want me to sing *with him?*

GREEN. Honey, you either sing like a friggin' canary or I'll bash the lead outta' ya'!

RED. Humphh!

BLUE. But what do we do if it doesn't work?

GREEN. Beats me, but I'd rather die tryin' than cryin'… *(looks around)*…everybody ready?

(…they all nod, except for **RED**, *who huffs…)*

Uh hum…Silent night…

GREEN, SILVER & GOLD. …holy night…

GREEN, SILVER, GOLD & BLUE. …all is calm, all is bright…

(…they stop and slowly turn to glare at **RED**, *who winces…* **GREEN** *and* **BLUE** *rock into her from either side…)*

RED. …'round young virgin, Mother and Child…

GREEN, SILVER, GOLD, BLUE & RED. …Holy Infant, so tender and mild, sleep in heavenly peace, sleep in heavenly peace.

(…their looks of concern melt into those of amazement…)

GREEN. Well, whatta' ya' know?

SILVER. That was close.

RED. Can't believe it really worked.

GOLD. They stopped breaking things.

SILVER. They're smiling again.

GREEN. They're kissin'.

RED. Oh, goody, looks like they're gonna' play the "chase me" game.

GREEN. *Without* the tree.

BLUE. There indeed appears to be a truce.

RED. For now.

GREEN. Sure hope it lasts.

GOLD. Me too, my tummy hurts.

SILVER. Look! She's coming over with the cover.

GOLD. They're putting us back!

BLUE. Reprieved!

RED. I'm gettin'…very…*(seductively)*…sleepy.

GREEN. Well, sweet dreams everybody…see ya' in nine months.

(…lights slowly fade into…)

(BLACKOUT)

SANTA COMES TO THE KING DAVID

(*SCENE: Exact center of Brooklyn Bridge.*)

(*TIME: Shortly before midnight, Christmas Eve.*)

(*AT RISE:* **MAN** *in Santa suit, staggers toward center of Bridge and, clearly out of breath, grasps his knees and tries to catch it. He then walks towards and climbs protective railing, leaning against it while reaching beneath his t-shirt, just as a* **WOMAN**, *wearing fuzzy slippers and a mink coat over pajamas, suddenly appears, sees* **MAN** *and gasps…*)

WOMAN Stop!

(*…startled* **MAN** *begins to wobble…*)

MAN. Ahhhh!

WOMAN. No!

(*…grabbing seat of his Santa pants, she yanks him back over railing and onto bridge…*)

MAN. What the…

WOMAN. …are you OK?

MAN. Who are you?

WOMAN. Relax, I won't hurt you.

MAN. Hurt me? You almost killed me!

WOMAN. You don't have to do it.

MAN. Do what?

WOMAN. Whatever happened, it's not that bad, it's not worth this.

MAN. What bad? What this?

WOMAN. Trust me, I know how hard rejection can be, especially around the holidays…

MAN. …excuse me, but…

WOMAN. ...*(but)* by this time tomorrow Christmas will be over...

> *(...she takes tissue from her coat...)*

MAN. ...listen, lady...

WOMAN. ...New Years will be right around the corner...

> *(...she dabs her eyes...)*

...then that will be over too...

MAN. ...lady...

> *(...her voice cracks...)*

WOMAN. ...and before you know it, so will the disappointment, the loneliness, the hurt, the...

MAN. ...lady!

WOMAN. What?

MAN. What are you talking about?

WOMAN. It's just that I'm feeling how much pain you must be in...

MAN. ...I'm not in any pain...

WOMAN. ...and I know that once we get a chance to talk things through...what do you mean you're not in any pain?

MAN. I'm not.

WOMAN. You're not?

MAN. Actually, up until this moment, I've never felt better.

WOMAN. You haven't?

MAN. Which was just what I was thinking before you came out of nowhere, grabbed me from behind and...

WOMAN. ...I was trying to save you!

MAN. Save me?

> *(...he leaps up...)*

Thanks to you, I almost wound up in the East River!

WOMAN. Isn't that what you wanted?

MAN. Why would I want to...

> *(...looking over railing, he laughs...)*

…wait a second, you think I was trying to…

WOMAN. …weren't you?

MAN. Are you nuts?

WOMAN. Oh my God, I almost killed you!

(…*she sobs as* **MAN** *climbs down and places a hand on her shoulder…*)

MAN. Hey, don't do that, it's alright…really…no harm done.

WOMAN. Everything I touch turns to sh…

MAN. …shhh, it's really OK, I didn't mean to snap at you like that.

WOMAN. Are you sure you weren't trying to kill yourself?

MAN. Think I'd know if I was.

WOMAN. Then what were you doing?

MAN. Keeping a promise.

WOMAN. Up here? On Christmas Eve?

MAN. That's what she wanted.

WOMAN. Your mother?

MAN. She's gone.

WOMAN. Your wife?

MAN. Not married…divorced…twice.

WOMAN. Your girlfriend?

MAN. Don't have one.

WOMAN. Child?

MAN. NYU…Freshman…next year…wanna' see her picture?

(…*he reaches for his wallet and flips it open…*)

WOMAN. Sure.

MAN. This is Margaret…somethin' else, isn't she?

WOMAN. She's beautiful.

MAN. An Angel…inside *and* out.

WOMAN. She's very lucky, not every girl can say her father is Santa Claus.

MAN. I'm the one who's lucky.

WOMAN. Alright, so if it wasn't Margaret, a wife, a girlfriend or your mother you made this promise to, then who…

MAN. …I'm not sure.

WOMAN. You were hanging over the side of the Brooklyn Bridge ten minutes before Christmas keeping a promise for someone you don't even know?

MAN. I know who it was, I just don't know if it really was who it was.

WOMAN. Are you OK?

MAN. I'm working on it.

WOMAN. And why are you dressed in a Santa suit?

MAN. It's Christmas Eve.

WOMAN. No kidding…but why the suit?

MAN. 'Cause I was Santa tonight.

WOMAN. *(sarcastic)* Really.

MAN. Really.

WOMAN. Macy's? Bloomies? FAO? K-Mart?

MAN. The King David.

WOMAN. Come again?

MAN. A nursing home up in Riverdale, right across the street from Van Cortland…

WOMAN. …I know what it is and where it is…so you're telling me you played Santa at a Jewish nursing home tonight.

MAN. I do every Christmas Eve…sort of a tradition.

WOMAN. How ecumenical of you…I don't get it.

MAN. It's because of Stella.

WOMAN. Who's Stella?

MAN. Stella Levy. She was my mom's best friend when we lived in the Bronx…where I grew up.

WOMAN. Your mother's best friend was Jewish?

MAN. Yeah…she and her husband Dave lived down the hall from us on the top floor of a five story walk-up on University Avenue. They were different from anyone else

I knew…cultured, civilized, kind…they owned an old Dumont radio that was always playing Dorsey, Jolson, Sinatra, Lanza, Rachmaninoff, Gershwin…stuff I'd never heard before but couldn't stop listening to. Hell, they even had a piano in their living room!

WOMAN. On the top floor of a five story walk-up?

MAN. Yup…a beautiful Steinway with a top so shiny you could see your reflection in it…and in the exact center of that polished piano top sat a box of chocolates – and inside that box was my favorite candy in the whole wide world…

WOMAN. …which was…

MAN. …a little square with three stripes, each stripe a different kind of…

WOMAN. …truffles!

MAN. That's it! How did you…

WOMAN. …my mother bought 'em too – they're Parve.

MAN. Parve?

WOMAN. Kosher…she kept a Kosher home.

MAN. Funny, so did Stella.

WOMAN. Yeah, funny.

MAN. So every day after school I'd stop by Stella's and as she let me in she'd always say "Go and get your candy, Timmy."

WOMAN. Finally I get your name.

TIM. Hey, that's right, I don't even know your…

WOMAN. …Marsha…Marsha Zimmerman…

MARSHA. …hi Timmy.

TIM. Timothy…Tim…Cleary…

> (…*he extends a hand, which she politely shakes…*)

…hi, Marsha.

> (…*she withdraws it…*)

MARSHA. So, of course, you'd always get the candy.

TIM. Of course…and it was always a brand new box I thought, because in the entire box there was only one slot for one truffle and every day I'd open it and there it would be, waiting for me...untouched...unwanted. Why no one else wanted this incredible prize always amazed me, but just in case, I'd run home from school every day in fear that someone might get wise and beat me to it...

MARSHA. ...but they never did, did they?

TIM. Never, 'cause what I didn't realize 'til years later was that Stella kept a separate box of truffles hidden away and would always replace the piece I had taken before I got there the next day.

MARSHA. Sweet.

TIM. That was Stella...there were times when her sweetness was all I had to look back on...to hold on to.

MARSHA. So what's all this have to do with promises and Santa suits?

TIM. Everything. When I was growing up, we didn't know from Jewish or Catholic...nobody did...Jews had their Catholic friends over for Chanukah, Catholics had their Jewish friends over for Christmas. For me, Christmas was like a second Halloween, because I'd always dress up like Santa and every time the buzzer would ring I'd run to the door, swing it open and bellow in my squeaky voice "Ho, ho, ho, Merry Christmas everybody, welcome to the North Pole," totally convinced I'd just pulled off the deception of the century. Eventually, Stella and Dave would arrive, and she'd stand at the open door, always act surprised, hand me one of those hollow chocolate Santas, bend down, kiss me on the cheek and say "How's Stella's little Santa." All was well with the world...Sholom, Pacem en Terra, Good Will Toward Men...

MARSHA. ...then...

TIM. ...children grow, fantasies fade, adults forget and unfortunately, so did I. But Stella's cards never stopped... followed me wherever I moved...sometimes they'd arrive a day or two late, but they'd always arrive. Aside from those cards and the occasional phone calls...

chance meetings…Dave's funeral…I let things slip away…let my life get in the way of being alive…being human. Throw in a couple of failed marriages, one great kid, some less than great career moves and… well, Stella and I just about lost touch. Then on Christmas Eve ten tears ago, I got a call from Stella's sister Lilly, telling me that Stella was at the King David and that she'd been asking for me. Next thing I knew, I was on the Cross Bronx…I was going home to Stella. Suddenly, this wacky idea hit me, so I swerved onto Jerome Avenue, booked up to Fordham Road and drove around until I found a novelty store that sold a Santa suit, which I bought, threw on, and high geared it to the King David.

MARSHA. Stella's little Santa.

TIM. Exactly. Her sister was waiting there when I drove up and took me to Stella's room. I walked in and there was this woman staring out the window…she turned and…I couldn't believe my eyes, Marsha, she was an old woman…for some reason, I never thought of Stella getting older, as someone who could even *get* older, yet there she was, a wrinkled smile screaming out "How's Stella's little Santa?" She reached out to me… we hugged…then she took something out of her robe and handed it to me – truffles – it was a box of truffles…"Go ahead, take your candy, Timmy," she said. I did. It felt like I was back in her home. I felt wanted again…understood…cared for…loved. Then while we were there, the craziest thing started to happen.

MARSHA. What?

TIM. All these old timers started shuffling into Stella's room. One by one they came up to me and started pulling on my suit…calling me Santa and whispering in my ear…asking me for things.

MARSHA. What kind of things?

TIM. Dolls, cap guns, roller skates, sleds, you name it…it was like they'd all become little kids again…then Stella looked at me and said "Go on, Santa, they're waiting for you."

MARSHA. What did you do?

TIM. I asked the nurse if there was a place we could go, so she led us all to the cafeteria and that's where we set it up.

MARSHA. Set what up?

TIM. The Chanukah bush.

MARSHA. And where did you manage to find a Chanukah bush?

TIM. Let's just say I liberated a ratty looking, half dead evergreen from the wasteland the Home called a garden… added a few busted candy canes, some Christmas balls cutout of construction paper, strung a little popcorn, threw a handful of cotton balls in strategic locations, topped it off with a Star of David and…voila! Instant Chanukah Bush.

MARSHA. Only a goy would say that.

TIM. Oh, and I almost forgot about my Santa chair.

MARSHA. Your Santa chair?

TIM. Sure…drape a little red chintz over a metal folding chair…perfection!

MARSHA. Oh.

TIM. Like I said, they were just like children…imaginations requiring minimal illusion.

MARSHA. I see.

TIM. And just like that we had our very own North Pole.

MARSHA. In the cafeteria of the King David Nursing Home.

TIM. You'd be surprised how many eighty year old Jewish grandmothers and grandfathers secretly want to sit on Santa's lap and tell him what they want for Chanukah…you should've seen the line…just like Macy's.

MARSHA. Hebrew style.

TIM. And that's the way I've spent every Christmas Eve since…a visit with Stella, then down the hall to the cafeteria…until tonight, that is.

MARSHA. And what made tonight different from all other nights?

TIM. Until I got to the nursing home, nothing. Arrived at about the usual time, parked in the same spot...said hello to Charlie the guard at the front desk and went straight to the cafeteria to drop off my boxes...just like every other year...

MARSHA. ...except?

TIM. Except something felt different. Strange. It was quiet... too quiet. Everyone was acting weird, distant...

(...spotlight upstage left on a scrawny bush covered with tinsel, Christmas balls cut out of construction paper, strung popcorn, and topped by an aluminum foil-covered coat hanger bent into a Star of David – gift-wrapped boxes covering its base. To the left of the bush is a metal folding chairs covered in red chintz. **STELLA,** *a barefoot, white nightgown-dressed* **WOMAN** *appearing much younger than her mid 80's, gracefully enters from the wings, passes chair, and approaches* **TIM** *from behind, just as he positions gift boxes around the tree...)*

...but I blew it off and began arranging my gifts, when suddenly somebody tapped me on the shoulder...

(...she does...a startled **TIM** *turns around...)*

...Stella!

STELLA. Ahhh, there's my little Santa!

*(...***STELLA*** *wraps her arms around him...)*

TIM. You look so beautiful...so happy.

STELLA. I am...come over here.

(...taking his hand, she leads him to chintz-covered chair...)

Come...sit.

(...sitting him down, she slides onto his lap with the grace and innocence of a little girl...)

TIM. Are you OK?

STELLA. I've never been better…Timmy, I need a very special gift from Santa this year…a special favor.

TIM. Of course…anything.

(…reaching into her robe, she pulls out necklace that's draped around her neck, at the end of which dangles a broken heart friendship charm…)

A heart.

STELLA. Look closer, Timmy…only half a heart. My Davey wore the other half…nothing fancy, mind you, he bought them at the five and dime, but it's the most valuable thing I've ever owned…handed it to me when I was just sixteen…at the very center of the Brooklyn Bridge, no less. We promised each other we'd wear them for as long as we could, but that when our time had come, each of us would try to pass along our half to someone who hadn't been lucky enough to find what we had found – our other half, our beloved, our "bashert."

(…she removes necklace and begins to drape it over his neck when he stops her…)

TIM. No.

STELLA. What's wrong?

TIM. Look at you, you've never looked better. You won't be letting go of this for a long, long time.

STELLA. You said you'd do anything, didn't you?

TIM. Yes, I did, and I will, but…

STELLA. …but?

TIM. *(boyishly)* Alright…tell me what it is.

(…smiling, she stands, grabs his hand, pulls him off chair and leads him downstage toward imaginary window that she looks up at moonlight through…)

STELLA. Promise me you'll take this necklace to the same place where Davey handed it to me…where everything began for us…then slip it off, hold it out over the water…*(she holds it up)*…high up to the moonlight and who knows? Someone as beautiful as you might see the reflection and be drawn to it…drawn to the place where a wonderful thing once happened for us and where a wonderful thing may happen again, only this time to you, my darling boy…

(*…she slowly drapes chain around his neck and tucks it beneath his shirt…*)

…so promise me…promise me *now*.

TIM. I promise…but how will I know what to do after that?

(*..leading him back to chair, she sits him down…*)

STELLA. You'll know what to do…you'll know.

(*…she slides onto his lap…*)

STELLA. Remember, Timothy, sometimes it takes two broken hearts to make one whole.

(*…wrapping her arms around his neck, she rests her smiling face against* **TIM***'s chest…*)

TIM. Don't mean to play the Grinch here, Stella, but I don't think you realize how unusual your relationship was… jeez, most of us will never get a glimpse of what you and Dave had, much less…Stella?

(*…he shakes her…*)

Stella? Stella!

(*…he shakes her again…she's limp in his arms…*)

Holy…Stella, are you OK? Help! Somebody help us here!

(*…clutching her to his body, he stands, rips chintz off chair and shakes it onto floor where he carefully sets her down…he places his face next to her nose, feels for a pulse and heart beat, stands and quickly runs cross stage as* **STELLA***, bush, chair and boxes fall into darkness…*)

TIM (*continued*) Please! Somebody help us!

(*…***NURSE*** *suddenly enters…*)

NURSE. Whoever's making that racket, please try to…Mister Cleary, it's you.

TIM. Hurry, please, something's wrong.

NURSE. Wrong? What could be wrong?

>   (...*he drags her toward just relit bush, chair, boxes and outspread chintz,* **STELLA** *no longer on it...*)

TIM. Not what, *who*! Stella...Stella Levy.

>   (...*the* **NURSE** *stops...*)

NURSE. You don't know.

TIM. Know? Know what?

NURSE. I'm so sorry...somebody should have told you.

TIM. Told me what?

NURSE. She didn't suffer, I can promise you that.

>   (...**NURSE** *begins to cry...*)

TIM. What are you talking about? I was just...she's over here, right over here on the floor where I left her... don't just stand there, hurry, she needs your help, please help her, she's right over...

>   (...*he turns to see illuminated chair and boxes, without* **STELLA**...)

...I don't get it, she was there just a minute ago, right next to the boxes...

NURSE. ...I know this must be a shock for you, Mister Cleary...it was for us too...we were all taken by surprise...it happened only yesterday, just after midnight, but someone still should have called you.

TIM. It's alright.

NURSE. I'm very sorry you had to find out like this.

TIM. No, really, I'm fine...actually, I think I'm beginning to understand.

NURSE. It might help you to know that when I found her, she had the most glowing smile you could ever imagine...

TIM. ...that's because she's with Dave.

NURSE. Excuse me?

TIM. Nothing.

NURSE. Let me know if there's anything you need.

TIM. Yes…I will…thanks.

>*(…she exits…chair and boxes go dark as* TIM *turns toward relit* MARSHA…*)*

And that's what made tonight different from all the others.

MARSHA. Look how much she loved you…how much you loved her…it was so powerful you had to imagine one final meeting…one last chance to say goodbye to someone who…

>*(…reaching under his t-shirt,* TIM *removes, then extends, chain bearing* STELLA*'s dangling half heart, still draped around his neck…)*

…my God, how did you get that?

TIM. Weren't you listening?

MARSHA. Of course, but I thought you'd just imagined…

>*(…he holds out* STELLA*'s heart.)*

TIM. …this isn't my imagination and neither was my running through the lobby of the King David, out the doors and down the street…minute by minute, hour after hour, running five, ten, who knows how many miles, all the time hearing her words echoing through my head, over and over again until suddenly I realized what I was doing…knew where I was going…I was keeping my promise, my promise to Stella…so I kept running, harder and faster than before, until I reached the place she wanted me to reach…right here at the exact center of the bridge, when…

MARSHA. …*(when)* I showed up and interrupted everything.

TIM. Whatever "everything" is.

MARSHA. I'm sorry.

TIM. Don't be.

>*(…she looks out over water…)*

MARSHA. Thanks, Santa.

TIM. For what?

MARSHA. I was feeling pretty sorry for myself before I got here.

TIM. Why?

MARSHA. Why? 'Cause I was just about to celebrate one more in a string of lousy holidays when I finally figured out it would be better to spend it alone than with someone who just made me *feel* alone…so I ran too… fast as I could…jumped into my car and drove…drove to the quietest place I could think of…away from everything and everybody…a place where I could finally work some things out…start to find myself again…feel myself again…remember what feeling felt like.

TIM. And that place would be here?

MARSHA. Yeah, and right now, all of a sudden, I'm feelin' pretty damn smart – *and* lucky.

TIM. Me too.

> (*…they draw close, lips almost touching, when CHURCH BELLS suddenly peel…it's midnight…she pulls away…*)

MARSHA. Merry Christmas, Timothy.

TIM. Happy Chanukah, Marsha.

> (*…stepping away from each other, they turn and begin walking away…after a few steps, they turn back…*)

TIM & MARSHA. Listen, I…

> (*…they laugh…*)

MARSHA. …look, Santa, I don't know what your sleigh situation is, but my car is right over there and I really wouldn't mind dropping you off somewhere, so…

> (*…she begins removing her keys, but they stick in her coat pocket…*)

…damn!

TIM. What happened?

MARSHA. This stupid key chain's always getting stuck!

TIM. Let me try.

(*…he reaches into her coat pocket…*)

MARSHA. Careful, don't cut yourself, it's cracked.

(*…there's a snapping sound…*)

TIM. Nuts! Think I just broke it.

MARSHA. No big deal, it's just a cheap piece of plastic.

(*…finally removing her keys, he sees they're attached to a key chain shaped like a large plastic heart, now cracked in half…*)

TIM. Holy…

MARSHA. …what's wrong?

(*…reaching into his Santa suit, he pulls out Stella's broken heart charm, extending both it and Marsha's broken key chain up to moonlight…they stare at the reflecting broken hearts, then each other…*)

TIM. What do we do now?

MARSHA. Stella said you'd know what to do…

(*..she reaches out and touches the necklace…*)

I believe her…don't you?

(*…**TIM** stares at hearts, then at **MARSHA**…he offers her his arm…*)

TIM. Ms. Zimmerman, would you afford me the pleasure of your company over a cup of holiday cheer?

MARSHA. I would be honored, Mister Claus.

(*…she accepts his arm…they stroll off as bells peel and lights fade into BLACKOUT.*)

Finis

PROP/COSTUME LIST

THE OFFICE PARTY

<u>STAGE PROPS</u>
- Couch

<u>COSTUME/PERSONAL PROPS</u>
- Santa Suit
- Male and female street clothes and underwear
- Gym bag

<u>SFX</u>
- Sound of car pulling up, door closing, car pulling away

SANTA'S CLARA

<u>STAGE PROPS</u>
- Bottle Redemption Machine (Painted refrigerator box with hole cut out
    to accept bottles, the words REDEMPTION CENTER lettered across it)
- Flat Bench (strong and long enough to hold Santa)
- Two garbage cans (one for clothes, one for trash; edible food planted
    in trash can)
- Bouquet of roses

<u>COSTUMES/PERSONAL PROPS</u>

SANTA
- Two Santa costumes (One story book, one ratty and stained)
- Ratty Santa sneakers for wearing
- Old Santa sack filled with plastic bottles
- At least 3 pair of sneakers tied together by the laces, long enough for
    Santa to drape around his neck (need not match)
- Wire-rimmed glasses
- Whiskey botde
- One pair of new red sparkle sneakers for Dawn
- Yellowed photograph

DAWN
- Clothes are worn, weathered, grunge type
- Back pack
- Large plastic bag or shopping cart for plastic bottles

KID
- Typical street kid clothes
- Large plastic bag for empties

THE FIRST NOEL

COSTUME/PERSONAL PROPS
- Coat, wool cap, scarf, pants & sneakers, finger-less mittens.
- Corrugated cardboard sign, the words HOMELESS FOR THE HOLIDAYS
    markered across it, twine attached at top corners long enough to
    drape over head

- Used coffee cup, several very wrinkled dollar bills and some change planted in it
- Foam take-out container, planted inside coat

BALLS

<u>STAGE PROPS</u>
- Oversized Angel ornament wing
- Oversized knotted ball of tinsel

<u>COSTUMES</u>
- Ball costumes can be as simple or elaborate as budget allows, but should be character color-coded, shiny material without arm holes, could have an opening at the bottom that allows entering stage, but will cover legs/feet when characters are sitting. If possible, costumes should be as close to ball shape as possible. Caps can be inverted pie tins with wire loops attached and elastic chin straps. A large candy cane should protrude from Gold's costume.

<u>SFX</u>
- Sounds of breaking glass

SANTA COMES TO THE KING DAVID

<u>STAGE PROPS</u>
- Platform suggesting ledge of Brooklyn Bridge -Bridge walkway resting bench .
- Chanukkah bush: small, scrawny tree covered with tinsel, Christmas Balls cut out of construction paper, strung popcorn, and topped by aluminum foil-covered coat hanger bent into Star of David.
- Gift-wrapped boxes -Metal, red material-covered, folding chair

<u>COSTUMES/PERSONAL PROPS</u>

TIM
- Santa suit
- Pea coat or similar
- Wallet

MARSHA
- Pajamas
- Fuzzy slippers
- Faux mink coat
- Key chain with large plastic half-heart attached
- Tissues

STELLA
- Nightgown -Necklace with half-heart silver charm

NURSE
- Nurse outfit

<u>SFX</u>
- Church bells

ABOUT THE AUTHOR

GEORGE CAMERON GRANT is an internationally produced author of eight full length plays, over twenty one acts, and numerous monologues. His latest one act play PUSH joins EPITAPH, a full-length play dedicated to his Father, and 4 X'MAS, his evening of one-act Christmas plays, as published members of the Samuel French family. He is an eight-time Samuel French Off Off Broadway Short Play Festival Finalist, most recently in 2009 for his play FORECLOSURE, which was also named a Finalist in the Nantucket Short Play Festival. PUSH was a Semi-Finalist in NYC's 2011 Strawberry Festival, garnering Best Actress and Best Director nominations. The Eastside Players of Madison (WI) High School entered PUSH into the 2012 Wisonsin High School Theatre Festival, receiving an All-State Award, and an Outstanding Actor Award for Scout Slava-Ross' portrayal of Eve. LEBEN, his full-length taking on pro-life/pro-choice issues, had its West Coast Premiere September 2012, at the Stage Door Repertory Theatre in Anaheim, CA. His new full-length Christmas play, HEAVEN CENT, written on commission for the same theater, had its World Premiere there on November, 2012, and was called "ONE OF THE YEAR'S 5 BEST" by Angela Hatcher of the Orange County News.

As Bookwriter/Lyricist/Composer, George recently completed a hugely successful series of staged readings of IN SEARCH OF ALICE, the second original musical he has created in collaboration with New York composer Michael J. Shapiro.

Also a two-time participant in the NY Independent Film Market, George has just completed his fourth screenplay DOUBLE EXPOSURE.

Composer of dozens of songs, George's PASS ON THE LOVE, performed by the legendary Persuasions, was featured in Spike Lee's DO IT A CAPPELLA.

George is an Addy Award winner for his graphic design work on August Wilson's FENCES, also creating for scores of motion pictures, including Academy Award® Winners and Nominees including ANVIL-THE STORY OF ANVIL, MONSTER, Y TU MAMA TAMBIEN, WHALE RIDER and AMADEUS.

George is the proud father of Elizabeth and Jenna. He is a member of BMI and the Dramatists Guild.

He can be reached on Facebook, Twitter: @cameron313, email: cameron313@aol.com or at www.georgecamerongrant.com.

Also by
George Cameron Grant...

Push

Epitaph

OTHER GEORGE CAMERON GRANT TITLES AVAILABLE FROM SAMUEL FRENCH

PUSH
GEORGE CAMERON GRANT

Drama / 1m, 1f, 3boy(s), 3girl(s), 1m or f / Bare Stage
What would it take to push your child over the edge? Eve, a 16 year-old girl, has fallen asleep in the darkened, dingy corner of a deserted subway station, not far from the platform edge where Billy, her 18 year-old brother, chose to leave this world, and where she'll soon struggle to find the reasons NOT to follow him. ONE BULLIED CHILD IS ONE TOO MANY!